Flirting Practice
Session #1

"Look," said Pam, pointing at two guys sitting on a bench. "Let's start with them."

My stomach flip-flopped. Couldn't we wait another two minutes? I wondered anxiously.

"We'll go stand over there," said Pam. I followed her. Neither of us looked at the guys as we passed, but Pam stopped near them. I felt really stupid.

"Okay, now we have to let them know we're interested," she said. "Let's look at them. Ready? One, two, three—look." I turned toward the guys. They were looking right at us. This is so embarrassing! I thought.

I caught the brown-haired boy's eye. He smiled. I looked away. Pam laughed. "It worked!"

"Shhh!" I said. "They'll know we're talking about them."

"That's the whole point," Pam said. She looked at them again. I peeked out of the corner of my eye. This time Pam smiled. They both smiled back. "This is kind of fun," she said.

Other Bullseye Books you will enjoy

Getting Even by Mavis Jukes
The Real Me by Betty Miles
The Tiny Parents by Ellen Weiss
  and Mel Friedman
The Trouble with Thirteen by Betty Miles
What It's All About by Norma Klein

Marci's Secret Book of Flirting

Don't Go Out Without It!

Jan Gelman

Bullseye Books   Alfred A. Knopf
New York

DR. M. JERRY WEISS, Distinguished Service Professor of Communications at Jersey City State College, is the educational consultant for Bullseye Books. A past chair of the International Reading Association President's Advisory Committee on Intellectual Freedom, he travels frequently to give workshops on the use of trade books in schools.

A BULLSEYE BOOK PUBLISHED BY ALFRED A. KNOPF, INC.
Text copyright © 1990 by Jan Gelman
Cover art copyright © 1990 by Dominick Finelle
All rights reserved under International and Pan-American Copyright Conventions. Published in the United States by Alfred A. Knopf, Inc., New York, and simultaneously in Canada by Random House of Canada Limited, Toronto. Distributed by Random House, Inc., New York.

Library of Congress Cataloging-in-Publication Data
Gelman, Jan. Marci's secret book of flirting : don't go out without it! / Jan Gelman.   p.   cm. (Bullseye books) Summary: Determined to learn how to attract boys, seventh grader Marci and her friend Pam decide to do a serious study of flirting and keep the results in a notebook.   ISBN 0-394-81931-4 (pbk.) ISBN 0-394-91931-9 (lib. bdg.)   [1. Interpersonal relations—Fiction.   2. Schools—Fiction] I. Title. PZ7.G2836Mar   1990   [Fic]—dc19   89-2439

RL: 4.5
First Bullseye edition: January 1990

Manufactured in the United States of America
1   2   3   4   5   6   7   8   9   10

To Marla Salzman, for all the laughs we had testing flirting techniques, and to Denna Sobke, Pam Weber, and Trudi Johnson, Terri Thomas, and the rest of my friends at The Vail Trail.

Marci's Secret Book of Flirting
Don't Go Out Without It!

Dear Cathy,

Boys are a pain. They steal your note-books at school and try to pull down your bathing suit at the beach. Besides, I never know what to say to them.

Sisters are a pain too. Especially when they're sixteen, like Darlene. Every guy who sees her falls in love with her.

But the biggest pain of all is junior high school, and I don't even start until tomorrow. I think I'm scared. It's such a big school.

What do you wear on the first day? Pam says that since we're almost thirteen, we should look mature. I'm not really sure what that means, but I've been trying to find clothes that make me look mature for the last two hours. I think it's hopeless. For

*now, I've settled on my blue dress with
the V neck.*

*Life was so much easier when I was eight
years old and you used to baby-sit me.
Sometimes I wish I was still eight. And I
wish you were still living next door—or at
least in California. Colorado seems so far
away. Why can't Darlene be away at college
instead of you?*

I'll write more later.

*Love,
Marci*

I put the letter on my night table and stood facing
my mirror. My blue dress drooped down over the
place where my hips were supposed to be.

I turned sideways and stuck out my chest. It
wasn't fair. These days everybody else had something to fill out their dresses. How come I didn't?

I picked up a black belt and buckled it around
my waist. My bedroom door flew open. It was my
best friend, Pam.

"What do you think?" I asked. "Should I wear
this tomorrow?"

Pam stood there, thin, blond and beautiful.
"Marci, if you get that dressed up, everyone will
know you're a seventh grader," she scolded.

She sank down on my bed on top of a pile of
pants, skirts, shirts and dresses.

"That dress simply must go!" she announced.

That's one thing about Pam. She's not afraid to say what's on her mind. She always gets straight to the point.

"Marci!" My five-year-old brother, Timmy, walked into my room. "You promised to come look at my new spider."

"Not now, Timmy. I'm busy."

"But Marci, it's black and green and has long furry legs."

"I'll come look *later*," I said, nudging him toward the door.

"Blaaah!" Timmy yelled, and jumped at me. "I'm going to catch you in my web and eat you!"

"Get out!" I shouted, chasing him with my fishing pole.

"Now, where were we?" asked Pam. She was used to Timmy. She picked up a black miniskirt and a pink button-down blouse. "Try this on."

After another hour Pam and I agreed on an outfit. I would wear my gray miniskirt, a white-and-gray-striped shirt, a white belt, gray socks and my white high-tops. At first we couldn't decide between my pink shirt and the white-and-gray one, but Pam said that white and gray made me look older, so we went with that.

"You look fabulous!" Pam said as I walked her to the door. "No one will ever know you're only in the seventh grade!"

"I'll see you at the bus stop at eight fifteen tomorrow morning," I said. "Thanks for the help."

The phone rang as I walked into the kitchen. I ignored it. It was probably for Darlene. Boys were always calling her. I opened the refrigerator and took out the spaghetti left over from last night's dinner. I found a clean fork in the dishwasher and ate a mouthful of spaghetti. My mom makes the best tomato sauce.

"Marci, your father is on the phone," Darlene said.

He's her father too, of course, but she doesn't talk to him.

"Make it quick. I'm expecting a call," she added.

It had been six months since Dad moved out of the house to San Diego. Mom said that it was the best thing for both of them. Los Angeles was only two hours from San Diego, but I felt as though I didn't have a father anymore. I wasn't as mad about the divorce as Darlene, but I was pretty angry. He keeps in touch by phone, but it's not the same as having him in the house. I miss him, even though he could get angry about the littlest things.

"Hi, sweetheart!" my dad said. "How's my seventh grader doing?"

"Okay, I guess." I didn't want to tell him that I was scared about going to the new school.

"I wanted to call you and wish you good luck on your first day," he said. "You remember my partner, Bob, don't you?"

"Sure," I lied.

"He just moved to Brentwood and his son will be in your school. You should look him up."

The last time my father made me meet some friend's son, I thought I was going to die. His ears stuck straight out like an elf's and he spilled his whole plate of pork and beans all over me at lunch. What a nightmare!

Dad started to ask me how Darlene was doing, but I didn't want to talk about it. I knew he was hurt because Darlene wouldn't talk to him, but I just didn't want to get involved. Dad always wants to know what's going on with her, but she won't talk to him. She's still angry about the divorce. So I get stuck in the middle. "I've got to run, Dad," I said.

"Okay, honey. Call me tomorrow and tell me how things went."

Timmy was tugging on my arm. "Bye, Dad! Thanks," I said.

"Hi, Daddy!" Timmy said as soon as he had grabbed the phone out of my hand.

I picked up my bowl of spaghetti and walked into the den.

"It's really big, you wouldn't believe it!" Timmy said into the phone. The divorce never seems to affect Timmy. He talks to Dad all the time as though nothing's changed. I wish I could feel that way.

"Marci won't even look at it," he said.

Oh brother, I thought, rolling my eyes.

"Bye, Dad. I'll tell her," Timmy said. He giggled.

I ate a forkful of spaghetti. Timmy marched into the den.

"Daddy said that you have to come look at my spider!" He grabbed my arm. "Come on!"

"Let go of me!"

"No, come on." He pulled me toward him.

"Stop it!" I shouted. But it was too late.

I lost my balance. The spaghetti flew out of the bowl and landed all over me. My mature-looking white-and-gray shirt was now covered with Mom's wonderful tomato sauce.

P.S. Brothers are a pain too!

"I thought we agreed on the gray-and-white outfit," Pam said when I arrived at the bus stop in my pink shirt.

"Hey, guys, listen up," Leslie Weber said as she walked toward us. "You're not going to believe this!"

Pam quickly forgot about my clothes. Leslie always knows everything that goes on in town, and she loves to gossip. My mother told me that Leslie's mother is the same way. They were on the same P.T.A. board. When my parents decided to get a divorce, my mom wouldn't even go near Mrs. Weber. She said she didn't want her personal life broadcast to the world.

Leslie looked around. There were three guys and a girl standing near us. "Suzie Parker moved away!" she said, leaning over so only Pam and I could hear.

"So?" Pam asked. "What's the big deal?"

"The big deal," said Leslie, "is that Peter Johnson is now free for us!"

My heart jumped. Peter Johnson! Pam and I looked at each other and smiled. Last year we had decided that Peter Johnson was the cutest guy in the sixth grade. But he was going out with Suzie Parker, and we didn't have a chance.

"I wonder if he'll be in class with any of us," Leslie said.

"We'll find out soon enough," said Pam.

"How about us? Do we have any classes together?" Leslie asked.

We compared schedules. Leslie and I were in two classes together, and Pam and I had the same homeroom.

The bus finally came. It was filled with people I didn't know, so Pam and I slipped into the first empty seat. Leslie sat behind us.

"Are you nervous?" Pam whispered.

I nodded. "I wish we had at least visited the school," I said.

When we got off the bus, Pam and I started looking for the C building. It was like going through a maze. The buildings weren't in alphabetical order, and we must have wandered around in circles for at least fifteen minutes. Kids rushed by us in every direction. Pam didn't want to ask anyone where to go. She said if she did, they would know we were seventh graders. I didn't really want to ask anyone either. Everybody looked as if they knew exactly where they were going.

"How are we ever going to get to our classes on time?" I complained. "They only give us seven minutes to get from one to the other."

Pam shrugged her shoulders. "I have no idea."

We finally stumbled on Building C and found our homeroom. Pam and I sat next to each other and listened to the teacher talk about how important it was to be on time. Homeroom was boring, but at least we saw some familiar kids there from our sixth-grade class.

My first class was social studies. Pam had math. We made plans to meet at lunch.

I walked down a crowded hallway to get to my class. Voices and laughter echoed all around me. Junior high sure is different, I thought. The kids look so grown up! I felt incredibly young as I walked through the halls. I barely reached most of the kids' shoulders. And I passed girls who had figures like my mother's. I wondered if I'd ever look like that.

I found Building L and walked into Room 227. I sat down in the second row from the back. Leslie came in a few minutes later and sat down next to me.

"Guess what!" She leaned toward me.

"What?"

She glanced behind her and around the room. Then she moved her chair closer to me.

"Peter Johnson is in our science class," she whispered.

"How do you know?" She always amazed me. It was like she had antennas or something.

"He's in my homeroom and I looked at his schedule. Can you believe it? I think it's fate!" She sighed and put her hand on her heart.

Just then something wet hit me on the head. Yuck, a spitball, I thought. I turned around. Two boys were laughing in the corner. One of them was Jerome Willard, the biggest creep in my sixth-grade class. Last year, when I was wearing my favorite blue dress, he shook up his soda at lunch and sprayed it all over me!

I glared at Jerome.

"Gross!" Leslie suddenly screeched. The whole class turned around. "Someone threw a spitball at me!" she wailed. She pointed to the wad of wet paper that had landed on her desk.

A tall, dark-haired woman walked to the front of the room. "Boys, that's enough," she said sternly. "There will be none of that kind of behavior in this class."

Leslie turned around and smirked at Jerome. "That'll teach them," she whispered to me.

The rest of the period went by pretty fast. Our teacher, Mrs. Blume, spent most of the time telling us about a group project that we would be doing on American settlers. It sounded hard.

My last class before lunch was English. The teacher was ten minutes late, and she spent most of the period taking roll. At the end we had to fill out a standardized form.

"Put your name where it says 'name,' " said the teacher.

No, put your name where it says address, I thought.

"Next, write your phone number in the space provided," she continued. "And then write your address next to that."

Oh, brother, I thought, rolling my eyes. Does she think we're in the first grade or something?

When English finally ended, I went to the cafeteria to meet Pam. The actual cafeteria and food lines were under a cement roof, but most of the lunch area was outside. There were groups of kids sitting at the outdoor picnic tables, under trees and on the grass.

I sat down at an empty table, facing the sun. I hoped that Pam would get there soon. Everybody around me seemed to be involved in their own conversations.

Where is she? I thought. I took out my notebook and started writing a letter to Cathy. I knew I'd feel better if I did something to keep me busy.

I looked up and saw a brown-haired boy walking toward my table. Oh, God, I thought. What'll I do if he sits next to me?

He kept walking in my direction. He was gorgeous. I looked down so he wouldn't think I was staring at him. Then he sat on the bench right across from me. My heart started pounding.

"Hi!" he said. He was looking directly at me. He had bright blue eyes that sparkled in the sun.

I managed a "Hi."

He smiled. God, he even has beautiful teeth, I thought.

"Are you in the seventh grade?" he asked. I knew it! The stupid pink shirt gave it away. Everyone must know how young I am.

"Yes," I mumbled.

"Me too," he said.

I looked at him and smiled. He smiled back.

He sure is cute, I thought. He was still smiling. Oh no, what do I say now? My mind was blank. The harder I tried to think of something, the blanker it got. I couldn't think of anything. Why couldn't I be like Darlene? I wondered. She always knew what to say.

"Heads up!" someone yelled. A football flew toward my face. I screamed and ducked.

"I got it!" the blue-eyed boy said. He jumped up and caught the ball.

"Thanks," I said, happy to have something to say. But before I could get one more word out, another guy came running over. I recognized him from sixth grade.

"Hey, you want to play with us?" he said. "We're short one guy."

"Yeah!" my blue-eyed boy said. He glanced at me and sort of waved. "See ya," he said.

Suddenly Pam showed up. "Who was that? He was just fabulous!"

"I know!" I said. "And I couldn't think of a thing to say to him. I just sat there staring at the table."

"Well, I don't blame you," Pam said. "I couldn't talk to this gorgeous guy in my English class either. He sat right behind me, and before class started he asked me what elementary school I had gone to. I could barely get the words out to answer him. And then I just sat there and didn't say anything else. What's wrong with us? How are we supposed to go on a date if we can't even talk to guys?"

Pam thinks we should start dating in the seventh grade. I shivered at the idea. Alone with Blue Eyes? What would I say? What would I do?

"I wonder how old Cathy was when she went on her first date," I said out loud.

"I bet she'd know what to do," Pam said.

Leslie came trotting over. Pam and I dropped our conversation.

"There's the cutest guy in my math class," she announced, flipping her curly brown hair back with her hand. She kept talking about all the people in her classes until the bell rang. I had math next.

The teacher made us take a practice quiz on basic skills, and then we had to fill out a bunch of forms. What a yawn.

Cooking wasn't much better. We watched our teacher make muffins and listened to a lecture on safety in the kitchen. I was glad when that was over.

Science was another story. I wished that it would never end, and it was all because Peter Johnson sat right behind me! I couldn't believe it. I glanced at him quickly as he walked past me. When he looked right at me with his chocolate-brown eyes I thought I was going to die!

Leslie got to class late and couldn't sit by me. She passed me a note from the other side of the room.

Marci,

You are so lucky! He's so cute. I would just croak if I were you!

love,
me

I quickly crumpled up the note and stuffed it into my backpack. That Leslie! I could have killed her. What if someone had seen it? Even worse, what if Peter had seen it? Of course, Leslie didn't sign her name to it. Only *my* name was on the note.

I didn't talk to Peter at all, but at least I was close to him. If I turn around, I thought, he'll know that I like him. So I looked straight ahead the whole time.

After school I met Pam in front of the main office. My mom finishes work at three, so she was going to pick us up. I told her to meet us around the corner. I didn't want anyone to see me with my mom.

As we walked around the corner I suddenly saw the blue-eyed boy from lunch. He was standing with a blond guy I didn't know, talking to a tall, thin girl.

"Look!" I said, nudging Pam. "It's Darlene!" I noticed our car parked next to her.

The guys were looking at her as if she were a goddess. Then she caught sight of me.

"Marci!" she called. "Over here!" I froze.

"There's my little sister," Darlene said, and walked toward us. I wanted to turn around and walk the other way. "See you," she said, and waved to the guys.

"I needed the car, so I told Mom I'd come get you," she said. Pam and I followed Darlene to the car and climbed in. "Did you see that little blond boy I was just talking to?" she asked. I didn't answer. "That's my friend Susan's little brother. Do you know him?"

"No," I said. But I know Blue Eyes, I thought. Why did Darlene have to show up around *him*?

We drove to Pam's house in silence. "I'll get off here and walk home later," I told Darlene as we got out of the car.

"Suit yourself," Darlene said and drove away.

"I don't understand it!" Pam said when we got to her room. "No offense, but Darlene is not that pretty, Marci. How come all the guys fall in love with her? I think you're a lot better looking than she is. Even my mom thinks so."

"I don't know," I grumbled. "It's been that way since she was ten. I wish I knew her secret. What does she have? What does she do?"

"I've got it!" Pam cried. "Let's follow her when she's in action. Then we'll find out!"

"That's a great idea," I said. "When we learn her secret, all the guys will fall in love with us too."

"Darling Marci, will you marry me?" Pam giggled as she bent down on one knee.

"Oh, maybe later," I said. "I'm booked this week." We laughed.

"So, what's our plan?" Pam asked.

"How about Thursday?" I said. "Darlene does the shopping for my mom on Thursdays after school. We could follow her around the supermarket."

"The supermarket?" Pam stared at me. "What's she going to do in a supermarket? It's full of women."

"Believe me, wherever Darlene goes, she finds guys," I said. "I don't know how she does it, but that's what we have to find out."

"How to meet the perfect guy!" Pam said in a dramatic voice. "We're on a secret mission . . . and we shall not fail!"

My mom picked us up after school on Thursday, and we drove straight home. This was the big day.

"You two are mighty quiet today," she said. "Is anything wrong?"

I looked at Pam. "Uh, no, Mom. School was thrilling, as usual. I guess I'm just tired."

"Now, Marci, don't start in about school. It's only the first week."

I sighed. My mother gets upset when I put down school. She says that school is a privilege, and I should take advantage of it to the fullest extent . . . whatever that means. My mom just doesn't understand. It's not that I don't like school, because I really don't mind it. It's just that the first week is always so disorganized.

"Just wait until things get going, and then I'm sure your classes will be very interesting," she said.

"Sure, Mom. I'll wait." I didn't try to argue with her. It was easier just to agree.

I leaned back and went over the Darlene Mission in my head. Pam and I had planned it all out at lunch. We had decided to take notes as we followed Darlene through the supermarket so we would remember everything. Pam thought we should wear disguises, but I thought that was going too far.

I didn't want anything to go wrong. This day could be very important to our future as teenagers.

When we got to my house, Pam and I went right upstairs. We strolled past Darlene's room, and I peeked in. She was curling her hair. I took out my Darlene Mission notebook and wrote:

DARLENE MISSION
THURSDAY

1. CURL HAIR

I closed the book. We went into my room and shut the door. Darlene's room was right next to mine, so we had to be careful. Pam pointed silently to the closet. I nodded and followed her in. We always had our most private conversations in there.

"Okay," I said. "Let's review this one more time."

"First, we get the car keys," Pam said.

"Then we sneak into the car and hide under the blankets," I said. Mom always kept two blankets in the back part of our station wagon. "We hide out back there while Darlene drives and parks the car."

"Next, we wait about five minutes after she's gone into the market," Pam said.

"Right," I whispered. "And then we follow her in."

"Taking notes," Pam added.

"And then we get back to the car, under the blankets and safely home."

"Let's go!" Pam said.

"Marci!" my mom called. I practically jumped out of the closet.

"Yes, Mom?" I said, trying to sound calm.

"Do you want anything from the market? Darlene's going in a couple of minutes."

"Pick me up some Honey Nut Cheerios," I said. I turned to Pam. "I could buy them myself," I whispered. We both laughed.

"Darlene, why do you insist on curling your hair? You are only going to the supermarket," I heard my mother say.

"You never know who I might run into, Mom!" Darlene said.

Pam nudged me. I smiled.

"Well, the keys are downstairs. I'm going to do some reading in my room," Mom said.

"This is it!" I grabbed Pam's arm. "Come on!"

"Mom, we're going to Pam's!" I yelled. "See ya later." We rushed downstairs.

"Dinner's at six, hon," my mom called.

We ran into the kitchen and looked around. No one was there.

 22 ♥

"There they are," Pam whispered, and pointed to a set of keys lying on the counter.

"Let's go!" I said. I picked up the keys and we ran out the door.

The station wagon was parked in front of the garage. I tried the first key. It didn't fit. I tried the next one. It didn't fit either.

"Hurry!" Pam urged.

My fingers felt like rubber, and I couldn't control them. I could barely hold the key chain. My heart was pounding faster and faster.

The next key fit. I struggled to open the door. Pam leaned over and pulled it open. She jumped in.

"I'll be right back. I have to replace these keys!" I ran to the house.

I heard Darlene say "I'll be back soon!" as she came down the stairs.

I threw the keys onto the counter, zoomed over to the car and jumped in.

"She's coming," I whispered.

We dove under the blankets and lay still. My chest felt like it was going to explode. Pam giggled. I put my hand over my mouth. I always laugh when I'm nervous.

The door opened. We froze.

I could feel the vibration of the engine as Darlene revved it up. We were on our way!

The drive to the market seemed to take forever. Pam kicked me every time we went over a bump.

I tried not to laugh. Then, to make matters worse, I got the hiccups. I kept my head buried under the blankets and tried to hold my breath.

When I get the hiccups with my dad, he makes me stretch my arms up over my head and hold my breath while he helps me gulp down some water. It always works. Unfortunately, I was in no position to use that method now.

Finally the car stopped and the door opened. I heard Darlene say something to a guy, and then the door closed.

"Wow! She's already met someone," Pam whispered excitedly. "I hope we're not missing anything."

"Shhh!"

"I can't breathe," Pam groaned.

"Just be quiet," I whispered. "We have to wait five minutes."

I heard voices outside our window.

"Hey, hurry up with that one. We don't have all day," said one male voice.

"I'm hurrying. Chill out!" said another.

Pam nudged me. "Can't I just peek?"

"No! There's someone out there."

Suddenly the car door opened, and the first voice said, "Well, it's time to get this thing on the road." Then the motor started.

Oh, my God, I thought. The car is being stolen.

"Marci," Pam gasped. "What's going on?"

The car began to move.

"I don't know."

My heart was pounding. I was afraid to talk. What if the robber heard us? What if he had a gun? What would he do to us? I tried not to think about it. Pam grabbed my hand.

Suddenly the car jolted to a stop. I heard the door open but the motor was still on. Pam squeezed my hand. My palm was sweaty and hot.

Then the car started moving again. Slowly.

"Marci!" Pam whimpered.

All of a sudden there was a loud thundering noise on the top of the car. I grabbed Pam. Something crashed into the sides and the whole car vibrated.

"W-w-what's going on?" I stammered.

Something started rumbling. The noise grew louder.

"We're being attacked!" Pam screamed, and jumped up. "Let me out!"

I tore off the blankets and sat up.

The windows were covered with soapy suds, and there were big brushes banging against the sides of the car. Then, as we watched, a sheet of clear water washed over the windows.

Pam and I stared at each other. Of course! The car wash! It's right next to the Safeway market.

The car started moving again, slowly. Then it stopped. Two young guys opened the door.

"Hey, Jeff, look what I found!" one guy with big brown eyes said. He looked at us as if we were crazy. "What are you doing here?" he asked.

"We live here!" Pam said calmly. "What else would we be doing here?"

How embarrassing! I thought. I wanted to climb back under the blankets.

"Well, okay," said another guy with a slightly crooked nose and blond hair. "If you live here, I guess that makes me the maid. And I've come to clean your house."

He stood there holding a long tube that was attached to a big machine.

"Well," Pam said in her most dignified tone, "I guess we'd better do our shopping." She climbed over the seat and flounced out of the car. I followed, holding my head high and not looking at the guys.

"Bye, boys," Pam said airily. I wondered how she could keep a straight face.

We walked around the side of the gas station toward the supermarket. When we were out of sight of the car wash, Pam grabbed my arm.

"We're being attacked!" I cried, and we fell on the ground laughing.

4

After about five minutes we managed to calm down enough to continue with our plan. We walked through the sliding glass doors of Safeway and looked around the store. There was no sign of Darlene. I picked up a basket and we walked though the turnstile.

"Well, at least I got rid of my hiccups," I said.

"Now, Marci," Pam warned. "This is serious business!"

"I know, Pam. I know."

We came to the first aisle and peeked around the corner. No Darlene. We walked down to the end of the aisle.

Suddenly Pam pushed me. "She's right behind us!" she whispered hoarsely. We scrambled into the next aisle, bumping into each other and giggling hysterically.

"Where do we watch her from?" Pam asked.

"I don't know!" I said. Suddenly I couldn't remember any of our plans. "Shhh! Listen."

I heard giggling. It was Darlene. "Where?" she was asking.

A male voice answered. "I'll show you. Come on."

"Thanks," she said.

Pam and I ran to the end of the aisle and ducked behind the paper towel display.

Darlene strolled by with a young, nice-looking guy. He was wearing a nametag that said CLIFF.

We tiptoed behind them, ducking down an aisle every few seconds. As we peeked out from behind the crackers, we spotted Darlene turning down aisle 13.

Perfect. We had a direct view of her from behind the frozen-juice section.

"Here you go," said Cliff. "If you need any help, I'll be stamping the canned peas in aisle 9."

"Thanks, Cliff! You're a doll." Darlene flashed him a big smile.

Next she walked through the cereal section and picked out some Raisin Bran.

"Honey Nut Cheerios!" I said without thinking. "Don't forget Honey Nut Cheerios!" Pam put her hand over my mouth.

"Marci!"

"Sorry!"

We stood up to get a better look. A tall, good-looking guy was walking toward Darlene. Just as he came up behind her, she picked up a box of Wheaties and backed right into him.

"Oh, I'm so sorry," she said with a smile. "What a klutz I am."

"No problem," he replied. "Nothing's broken."

"Good thing," said Darlene. "I couldn't afford a lawsuit."

The guy smiled and said, "I can see the headline now: GIRL ARRESTED FOR ASSAULT IN CEREAL AISLE." They both laughed.

I opened the notebook.

2. BUMP INTO GUY
3. SMILE

After he left, we followed Darlene to the produce section and crouched behind the potatoes.

Darlene was staring at the pineapples with a puzzled expression. A young guy walked by.

She smiled straight at him. "Excuse me," she asked. "Could you help me?"

"Sure," the guy said.

Darlene pointed to the pineapples. "How do you tell if they're ripe?"

I couldn't believe my ears; she had taught me that years ago.

The guy smiled and picked up a pineapple. "If you can pull one of the top leaves out easily, then the pineapple is ripe," he said as he demonstrated.

I opened my book and wrote:

Just then someone tapped me on the shoulder. "Well, hello there, Marci and Pammy!" a woman said.

Pam and I were still scrunched down behind the potatoes. I leaped to my feet. It was Leslie's mother! The big gossip!

I looked to see if Darlene had noticed us. She was still busy talking to the pineapple guy.

"How are you girls doing?" Mrs. Weber said. "Are you helping your sister with the food shopping, Marci? I saw Darlene just a minute ago."

"Uh, uh, yes," I stammered.

"So how do you like junior high school so far?" she asked.

"It's just fine," I said.

Great, I moaned inwardly. Just what I want to be doing—having a friendly chat with the world's biggest gossip while we're supposed to be spying on my sister! This is going to ruin everything.

"Marci, we better go find those crackers," Pam said through clenched teeth. She tugged at my arm.

"Uh, right." I turned back to Mrs. Weber. "Nice seeing you," I said.

"Bye, dears!" she called. "Tell your mothers I say hello."

"We will," Pam assured her.

"Sure," I said under my breath, "I'll tell Mom

you said hello, just as soon as I tell her about this little spy operation we're running."

We walked slowly away from the produce, and then we took off down the next aisle. Darlene was already in a checkout line. We sneaked to the front of the aisle and leaned against the candy rack where she couldn't see us.

A guy walked up behind her in line. She turned and smiled at him.

"Hey, there. How's it going?" he asked her.

"Great, thanks. How about you?"

"Super," he said. "You live around here?"

"Not far. I'm Darlene."

"I'm Mark," said the guy, smiling.

I took out my notebook and put a star next to "smile."

"You have a beautiful name," he continued. "It's so unusual."

I scribbled furiously.

5. NAME MUST BE BEAUTIFUL AND UN-
   USUAL—CHANGE OURS

I closed the book.

"Quick!" Pam hissed. "She's almost checked out! We better get back!"

We ran to the other side of the store and crept along the wall. "Do you realize we've got to go back to the car wash and face those guys again?"

moaned Pam when we got outside. "It's *sooo* embarrassing!"

We walked toward the station wagon. The guy with the big brown eyes was drying off the car next to ours.

"Hi, girls!" he said. "Home so soon?"

"Hey, listen," Pam said, drawing him aside. "It's her sister's birthday, and we're in the process of surprising her. Could you, like, keep this a secret?"

"Sure," the guy said. "I've never seen you before in my life." He smiled.

"Thanks," said Pam.

"You better get in quick. Here she comes," the guy warned.

Pam and I jumped into the car and tumbled into the back. I pulled the covers over us and we lay still.

The ride home went quickly. We waited five minutes after Darlene had emptied the car. Then we got out, locking the door after us.

We ran all the way to Pam's house and collapsed on her floor.

"Thank God that's over," Pam said. "What did you write? I didn't see too much. Did you?"

"Well, all I know is that every time we turned around she was talking to another guy," I said. I opened my book.

1. CURL HAIR
2. BUMP INTO GUY

*3. SMILE
4. ASK QUESTIONS
5. NAME MUST BE BEAUTIFUL AND UN-
USUAL—CHANGE OURS

We read the list over a few times. We decided to try curling our hair sometime during the next week.

"We have to smile a lot tomorrow," Pam said, "and start asking questions. Let's practice with guys who don't matter until we're good at it."

"Okay," I said. "But do we have to ask dumb questions like Darlene did? I mean, that pineapple question really blew my mind."

"I can't ask a question that I already know the answer to." Pam shrugged. "I would feel so stupid."

"Me too," I said. "So we won't do that."

NO DUMB QUESTIONS

I wrote in the margin.

"Now, what are we going to do about our names?" I asked.

"Let's change them!"

"I'll be Tiffany," I decided.

"That sounds good," Pam said. "I'll be Danielle."

I glanced at my watch. "Oh no, it's almost six. I've got to get home."

Pam walked me to the front door. "See you tomorrow, Tiffany," she said.

"Take care, Danielle."

I ran all the way home, hugging my notebook to my chest. The guys were going to flip over our new names—I was sure of it.

My mother was in the kitchen. "Hi, hon," she said.

"Hi, Mom." I walked into the den. Timmy was on the floor, coloring. Darlene was watching TV.

"Hi, Marci," Darlene said.

"My name is no longer Marci," I announced. "I am Tiffany."

"Tiffany? Why would you want to change your name?" she asked.

"Because guys like longer names," I said carefully. I didn't want her to get suspicious.

Darlene shook her head and rolled her eyes. "Marci, names don't have anything to do with it!" she said. "If you want to attract guys, you have to learn how to flirt. It's just like any other skill. You have to practice it before you can be any good."

"Well, who doesn't know that?" I said quickly.

So that's how she does it, I thought as I raced upstairs to the phone in my mom's room. She obviously had every move in the supermarket planned out!

I was so excited I could barely dial Pam's number.

"Pam," I said when she answered. "I've got the

♥ 34 ♥

answer to all our problems! All we have to do is learn how to flirt!"

"I already *know* that," Pam said. "But how? What do we do?"

"I don't know," I said. "Maybe a dictionary would help. Look up flirting in yours and I'll look it up in mine. We'll talk tomorrow."

P.P.S. Please S.O.S. instructions on how to flirt. Pam and I are desperate! We followed Darlene around Safeway one day and she met tons of guys. I don't understand what she does. We're going to try smiling and curling our hair for now, but what should we do after that?

I sealed the letter to Cathy and gave it to my mom to mail when I left for school the next morning. I hope she writes back soon, I thought as I walked to the bus stop.

I was meeting Pam fifteen minutes early so we could go over our flirting definitions. I was pretty confused by what I'd read. Maybe she'd had better luck.

Pam was sitting on the sidewalk with her nose buried in a book when I got to the bus stop. "I'm lost," she said, handing the dictionary to me. I saw what she meant.

flirt: 1: To move in a jerky manner. **2:** To move erratically.

"What does *erratically* mean?" I asked. Pam shrugged her shoulders. I looked it up.

erratic: 1: Transported from an original resting place esp. by a glacier. **2:** Unconventional; eccentric.

Pam giggled. "It sounds more like science class to me," she said.
We tried mine next.

flirt: 1: To amuse oneself in light, playful courtship. **2:** To deal triflingly; toy. **3:** To move jerkily; dart.

"Try looking up *courtship*," Pam said.

courtship: The act, process or period of courting or wooing.

"Woo! Woo! Woo!" Pam chanted. I looked up *wooing.*

woo: 1: To seek the affection of, esp. with intent to marry. **2:** To seek to achieve.

"Woo! Woo!" Pam sang. "We're only twelve, and we're seeking to get married."

I opened my book and wrote:

FLIRTING MISSION

FRIDAY

Then I copied down all the definitions. After thinking a moment I added:

CONCLUSION: ACCORDING TO OUR DICTION-ARIES, WE MUST MOVE IN A JERKY, PLAYFUL MANNER WHILE LOOKING FOR HUSBAND MA-TERIAL. THIS FLIRTING MISSION DEFINITELY NEEDS HELP. CATHY BETTER WRITE SOON.

"I know! It's all in the hips," Pam said. "We've got to wander down the streets jerking our hips from side to side." She stood up and started swaggering down the road. I joined her.

"Here we come, boys." She laughed, whacking me with her hip. "Watch out! We're on a search for husbands."

"Well, what do we have here?" a male voice asked. We skidded to a halt.

There stood Jerome. "Here we come, boys," he squeaked, swinging his hips.

My face felt like it was burning up. I was so embarrassed, I couldn't speak.

"Oh, you're so stupid, Jerome," Pam said. "We're practicing for a play. Don't you know anything? Come on, Marci." She grabbed my arm and pulled me around the corner.

How does Pam come up with such reasonable stories? "Oh, Pam . . ." I started to moan the minute he was out of sight. "I have never . . ."

"What are you girls doing cowering back here?" Leslie asked us as she strolled over to us. "And what is that horror Jerome doing at our bus stop?"

Uh-oh! Leslie the mouth! Pam and I just looked at each other without saying a word. Luckily Leslie didn't ask us any more questions. She was more interested in gossiping.

"Well, I finally found out the name of the cute guy in my math class," she said. "His name is Dave."

I didn't even know who she was talking about, and I really didn't care. Our lives had just been ruined. Why did Jerome have to be at our bus stop today? I just knew he would tell everyone what he'd seen. He loved to gossip as much as Leslie. What if he told Blue Eyes? My chances would be ruined for sure.

Jerome smirked at us practically the whole way to school. We tried to ignore him.

As soon as the bus stopped, Pam and I bolted for the door. "See you later, Leslie," I called.

The morning went on forever. Jerome sat right behind me in social studies. "I'm going to have to sleep over at my dad's house more often," he whispered to me. "Your bus stop is much more interesting than mine."

I pretended I didn't hear him.

Pam and I met at our usual picnic table for lunch. Just as I pulled out my turkey sandwich, I saw Jerome again. He was standing near the building with Peter Johnson and the rest of the boys from our sixth-grade class.

"He'll never keep his mouth shut," I said to Pam. "What do we do? I just know he'll tell them." I covered my face with my hands.

Suddenly all the guys came toward us wiggling their hips. "Get your hands away from your face. Act like nothing's wrong," Pam said sternly. "Keep talking. And ignore them."

I couldn't help it. I had to look at them. "Stop staring at them. Keep your eyes on me," Pam said.

I thought I was going to die. "And so that was such an interesting time when we went to the store," I started to babble. "Wasn't it, Pam?"

"Oh, yes," she said as Peter sashayed by us. "And the cow jumped over the moon and then fell down. And if we keep talking, maybe they will go away," she said through clenched teeth. We kept our eyes glued to each other.

Jerome smiled at us as he walked by. I glared back. "Hey, baby!" he said in a high-pitched voice. "Here we come. Look out!" The rest of the boys laughed.

We tried to ignore him. I hate Jerome more and more every day, I thought. The boys kept walking until they were out of sight. My heart was pounding. Why do these things happen to us? I thought.

"Well, we're doing real well with our flirting so far," I muttered. "We've managed to embarrass ourselves beyond embarrassment."

"At least we got their attention," Pam said. "Besides, they looked even stupider than we did." I couldn't help laughing. She was right.

"Hey, isn't that your blue-eyed guy?" Pam asked. "He's talking to Leslie."

I looked over at the lunch counter. There was Leslie, flipping her hair back and laughing as she smiled at *my* blue-eyed boy. How dare she! I thought. My whole body stiffened. Friends aren't supposed to steal your crush!

Leslie waved good-bye to Blue Eyes and headed toward us. I turned away quickly. I didn't want her to know I'd been watching.

"Hi, girls," she said. "Did you see who I was talking to?" She rolled her eyes. "Dave. What a beautiful name."

She'd been talking about him this morning, I realized. She liked the same boy I did! And Leslie always got what she wanted. I knew it was hope-less now.

"Bye," Leslie said. "I've got to go." She strutted away.

"Leslie," I said. "What a horrible name."

I trudged silently up to my room when I got home. Darlene was in the kitchen with my mom. I didn't feel like talking to anyone, especially not my sister. How come she never had boy problems? It just wasn't fair.

She probably never had a friend steal the love of her life, either. I guess it didn't really matter now if I did learn how to flirt. I thought of Blue Eyes and sighed. He had sure looked interested in Leslie.

"Marci, is that you?" my mother called.

"Yes, Mom."

"Your father phoned a few minutes ago. He said he'll call right back."

"Fine," I said.

"Marci, what's the matter? Did something happen at school? Are you all right?"

"I'm fine, Mom." Except some creep saw Pam and me pretending to flirt and then told every single guy in the seventh grade, and my "friend" Leslie is a boy-stealer. Other than that, I'm fine.

"Well, if you want to talk, I'm here," my mom said.

I shut the door to my room and lay down on my bed. I suddenly felt very tired, but I just couldn't stop thinking about Dave. As I closed my eyes, the phone rang.

"Marci, telephone!" called Darlene.

I went into my mom's room and picked up the phone.

"Hi, Marci," said my dad. "How are you doing? How was school?"

"Fine."

"Guess what?"

"What, Dad?" I wasn't in the mood for a guessing game.

"It's time for us to go fishing again. The annual office deep-sea fishing trip is coming up. We'll have a great time, just like always. I can't wait!" He spoke really fast, the way he does when he gets excited.

"That's great, Dad." I tried to sound enthusiastic. Every year since I was little, we've gone on this fishing trip. But now that Dad had moved out, I couldn't get really worked up about it.

"It'll be great to spend some time with you," he continued. "And we'll be sure to catch the biggest fish; I just know it. We always do!"

Every year his business has a competition to see

who catches the biggest fish. My dad and I have won the last four years. Actually, the trip has always been fun, but right now I just wasn't in the mood. "That'll be great, Dad," I mumbled. "Really."

"Okay, hon. I'll call you as soon as I find out the definite dates. I love you. Bye."

"Bye, Dad." I hung up the phone and headed back to my room. The phone rang again. I turned around to answer it, but it stopped ringing.

"Marci, it's for you again," Darlene said from downstairs. "But hurry up. I'm waiting for Brett to call."

I picked up the phone. It was Pam. "I've got the answer to our problems," she announced. "I asked my mom how to flirt and she told me that it was hard to explain, but the best way to learn is to watch someone. Well, I told her that we already tried watching Darlene but that didn't give us enough to go on, so she said she'd rent us some movies with flirtatious actresses. What do you think?"

I had practically given up on the whole flirting idea. "You asked your mom?" I said incredulously. I could never ask *my* mom how to flirt. She'd probably want to know why I was asking or something equally embarrassing. Pam sure had a lot of nerve.

"Of course. Who else would I ask?" she said. "My dad? Now, come on, tell me what you think.

This'll be great. Can we use your VCR? Ours is broken."

"Yeah, I guess so," I said.

"Super. We'll do it tomorrow. I'll come over in the morning. Bye!" And she hung up. Sometimes I really admire Pam. She sure is persistent. Maybe we really will learn how to flirt, I thought.

Pam arrived at my house at ten-thirty the next morning with a box full of makeup and two movies. "Mom gave me her old makeup," she said, pulling out some bright blue eye shadow and a purple eye pencil. "I will make you bea-u-ti-ful," she added in a French accent.

"Ah, but *mademoiselle,* am I not already bea-u-ti-ful?" I asked.

"Yes, but we can do so much more, *ma cherie.*"

"This is good, *mon amie,* because I need so much more. If I am truly bea-u-ti-ful, Blue Eyes will fall in love with me." I fell backward onto the couch and called, "Where are you, my love?"

Pam jumped on top of me. "I'm here, I'm here," she crooned. We both laughed as we fell off the other side of the couch.

I rolled over and pulled myself up. "Okay, let's get serious. What movies did you bring?"

"*Gone With the Wind* and *Grease.* My mom said that Scarlett O'Hara is a great flirt. The movie is long, but she said we only have to watch the beginning to get the idea."

"Well, let's go, then," I said.

"Marci, aren't you forgetting something?"

"What?" I was confused.

"The notebook, Marci, the book. We can't start without it."

"Oh, that!" I ran upstairs to my room, reached under the mattress and pulled out the book. I had hidden it well.

"Hurry up!" Pam yelled. "*Gone With the Wind* is starting."

We settled in. I had a pen and Pam had the remote control. "Be ready to stop it if we need to," I said.

Gone With the Wind took place in the 1860s. In the first scene Scarlett O'Hara, a beautiful young woman, was seated on a porch wearing a full dress with petticoats. Two young men hovered over her. Then Scarlett walked up and down the porch. The two guys followed right behind.

"Quick, stop the movie," I said. "Rewind that part."

Scarlett tilted her head to the side. She raised her shoulder and fluttered her eyelashes. "That was great!" Pam exclaimed. "Did you see how those guys looked at her? Are you writing this down?"

I scribbled:

FLIRTING MISSION
SATURDAY

GONE WITH THE WIND
SCARLETT O'HARA—
1. TILT HEAD
2. SMILE
3. MOVE SHOULDERS
4. BLINK EYES
5. TURN AWAY

COMMENTS: SCARLETT IS DEFINITELY BEAU-
TIFUL, BUT I DON'T THINK THAT'S THE ONLY
REASON SHE HAD THE GUYS' ATTENTION. IT
SEEMED AS IF SHE WAS PLAYING A GAME WHEN
SHE WOULD BLINK HER EYES AND THEN TURN
AWAY. AND SHE STRUTTED AROUND THE PORCH
SMILING AT THEM.

Pam stood up and imitated Scarlett. "Perfect!" I
said as she glided back and forth. "You're a natural."

I joined her, tilting my head sideways and smiling. "Well, hello there, boys. How are y'all doing?"

Now Scarlett was sitting down at a barbecue,
surrounded by about fifteen guys. "Look at them!
Every single guy loves her. How come?" Pam asked.

"She smiles a lot. And she keeps looking at them
all the time," I said.

6. LOOK GUYS IN THE EYE
7. SMILE MORE

"I get too embarrassed to look at guys that way," Pam said. "Maybe we should practice." Pam looked me in the eye. "Hi, Peter. How are you today?" Then she smiled and fluttered her eyelashes.

"Just fine, Pam. Do you have something in your eye?"

"Come on, Marci. This is serious."

"Okay. I'm sorry."

Pam walked by me again, this time sort of wiggling her shoulders and tilting her head. I couldn't help laughing. "I'm sorry, Pam. I think it's the sweatpants and sweatshirt," I said. "Maybe you need more flirtatious clothes. Look at Scarlett. She's wearing a low-cut dress. We should try that, too."

"Okay, let's find something to wear. And then we'll watch *Grease*," Pam said.

We pressed the rewind button and ran upstairs to my room. Pam opened my closet. "We need sexy clothes," she said. "Which you definitely don't have. Let's look in Darlene's closet."

"But she'll kill me if she finds out," I said.

"All's fair in love and war," Pam pointed out. "And this is definitely war!"

"You're right," I said. "Let's do it." We scurried into Darlene's room and opened her closet.

"I'm wearing this." Pam held up a bright pink, V-neck dress. She slipped out of her clothes and put it on. The V neck drooped straight down, baring half her chest.

"What do you think?" she asked, throwing her shoulders back and her chin up.

"Perfect," I said. "That'll get some attention for sure."

I pulled out a black dress with buttons down the front. I slipped it on and stepped back. "It's you," Pam said. "But come here." She unbuttoned another button. "We've got to show some cleavage," she said.

"I don't have any," I pointed out.

"A minor detail."

Pam took off the pink dress and picked out a lavender skirt and a white off-the-shoulder top. "This is better," she said. "Now all we need to do is put on some makeup."

"What about *Grease?*"

"Let's try the makeup out first." Pam ran downstairs and came back with the box. "Come here."

"Just a little, Pam." I had only put makeup on once. It had made me look like a clown.

"Don't you worry. You'll look fabulous!" She took out some blue eyeliner. "My mom showed me how to do this. Now shut your eyes and hold still."

I did. "Ouch!" I yelled as she poked me in the eye. "Watch that thing. It's dangerous!"

Pam giggled. "I'm sorry. Guess I got carried away." She continued with the liner and then followed it with light blue eye shadow, pink blush and some light pink lipstick. "There!" she said. "You look beautiful!"

I looked in the mirror and didn't even recognize myself. The makeup looked kind of funny, but maybe I just wasn't used to it.

"This is great!" said Pam. "Now do me." I put the makeup on her following her directions. "You look so old," I said when I was finished. "Do I look that old?"

"We look at least sixteen," Pam said. "Let's get some shoes and go!"

"Go? Go where? I'm not going out in public like this!"

"Oh, come on. We'll knock 'em dead. We'll go have pizza at John's Pizzeria. No one we know ever goes there! Who could possibly see us?"

"Okay," I grumbled. "But you'd better be right."

"Just follow me." Pam walked downstairs with a wiggle.

I wrote my mom a note, and we locked up the house and walked to the bus stop around the corner.

After about five minutes the bus came.

"Everyone's staring at us," I whispered to Pam as we got on.

"You're just paranoid," she told me.

We reached our stop and walked to the pizzeria. Pam peeked in the door. She gave the all-clear sign.

We sat down at a booth near the corner. A

brown-haired boy got up and headed straight for our table. "Look, he's coming over," Pam whispered. "It's working!"

He stopped. My heart was pounding. "Hi, girls!" he said.

"Hi," we squeaked.

"How are you doing today?"

"Fine," Pam said.

"Great!" He reached in his pocket and pulled out a pad. "What can I get you?"

He was our waiter! How could we be so stupid?

"A small pizza with pepperoni and mushrooms," said Pam. "And two Diet Cokes."

As he walked away, Pam and I cracked up.

"Are we retarded?" she asked.

"We sure are!" I answered. Pam's face looked like a neon sign with blue and purple eye shadow, and her shirt was falling off her shoulder. She looked pretty funny.

"Oh, well," Pam said. "At least we're getting used to the new us."

Suddenly the front door opened with a crash. "What a game," a male voice said loudly. "We creamed them!" A bunch of guys laughed in response. I stiffened. I knew those voices.

"Pam," I whispered. "Can you see who that is?" I refused to turn around.

She turned her head sideways, quickly. "Oh no!"

"Who is it?"

"Don't look. It's all of them. Peter and Dave and Jerome and the rest."

"What do we do?" I said, panicked. "Do you think we can sneak out?"

"We just ordered a pizza."

"I'm not hungry! I'll die if they see us! Let's go."

"Well, hello there," came Jerome's voice from behind us. He sauntered over to our table. "And how are we today?"

"Fine, Jerome," Pam said.

"So, what's with all the makeup, Pam?"

I looked down, trying to hide my face. Meanwhile Pam was busy pulling up the shoulder on her shirt.

"Hi Marci, Pam," Peter said, joining Jerome. I barely looked up, mumbling a quick "hi."

"You have it on too!" Jerome exclaimed. "What is this? National Makeup Day or something?" I wanted to crawl under the table.

Pam looked right at him. "As a matter of fact it is," she said in her best know-it-all voice. "It's a regular national holiday."

"Come on, Jerome. Let's go," Peter said. "Let the girls celebrate their holiday in peace. I'm starved."

I cringed as they walked away. "No one we know ever goes here?" I threw at Pam. "I knew I shouldn't have listened to you! I can't believe this!"

"C'mon, act like you're having fun," she said.

"Maybe we should try out some of our flirting on them!"

"No way!" I practically screamed. "You can. I'm not."

"Chicken. I'm going to try out a smile on them." Pam looked over toward the boys. She smiled.

"Well?"

"No reaction," she said. "They really are clueless. Jerome is the only one who even noticed our new look. And he's a creep."

Our lunch took forever to arrive. When it came, we practically inhaled it. The boys didn't even look up when we left. I couldn't wait to get home.

When we got to my house, I opened the door quietly. If Darlene saw us in her clothes, we were dead! But the coast was clear. We ran up to my room and locked the door. I took off Darlene's dress and slipped into my jeans.

"So, what do you think?" Pam said. "Was this a bust or what?"

I took out our secret book.

FLIRTING EXPEDITION #1: JOHN'S PIZZERIA

WE WERE CAUGHT AT THE PIZZERIA BY JEROME, DAVE, PETER AND THE REST WHILE WE WERE DRESSED TO THE MAX AND COVERED IN MAKEUP. WE AREN'T SURE IF THE GUYS ARE DENSE OR IF THEY JUST MATURE LATE, BUT

DRESSY CLOTHES AND MAKEUP DEFINITELY AREN'T THE ANSWER. WE'VE RUN OUT OF IDEAS. OUR LAST HOPE IS CATHY. MAYBE SHE'LL KNOW WHAT TO DO NEXT.

The next few weeks in school were busy. My social studies teacher handed out a list of ideas for projects on American settlers, and I chose a project about pioneers moving West. I had to draw a map showing the best route for the settlers to take across the country. On the map I had to show the natural obstacles they would run into, like mountain ranges, winter storms and rough terrain. I also had to mark the areas where different Indian tribes lived. And with the map I had to hand in a written paper describing the settlers' journey. I had never done anything so complicated in my life!

I went to the library the next day and took out six books for the project. When I got home, I settled on the floor in my room, surrounded by pages of maps, stories, historical accounts and biographies. I read my assignment over and over.

Where do I begin? I thought. There's so much to read. I'm never going to get this done.

My mom peeked in my room. "Hi, hon," she said. I looked at her helplessly. "What's the matter?" she asked.

I explained my project to her. "Let's take this one step at a time," she said.

For the next two hours we sat in my room, looking through books and talking about American settlers. "Remember," she said, "there were no microwaves back in those days. It was true campfire-style cooking." I laughed.

Timmy poked his head in my room. "Mom, when's dinner?"

"Oh, my. I completely lost track of time," my mom said. "I'd better start the campfire."

"Campfire?" Timmy looked puzzled.

"Nothing, dear." She smiled at me and got up. "Come help me get dinner started, Timmy. Your sister has lots of work to do."

"Thanks, Mom," I said. She had made my project sound kind of fun. I picked up one of the books, climbed onto my bed and propped a pillow up against my headboard. I leaned back and began to read.

For the next two weeks the project was all I thought about. Every day at lunch I would go to the library and work on the written part. And at home my mom helped me organize the map. Colored pencils, tracing paper and markers were strewn all over my floor.

Pam was amazed at how hard I was working.

"You mean I get a whole lunch period with you?" she teased one day when I decided to take a break from working.

After school she filled me in on the lunchtime gossip I had missed. Leslie kept her updated.

"Leslie's been talking to Dave more and more," Pam told me one day.

"Great," I said. "There go my chances."

"It might not mean anything," she said, trying to console me.

"Yeah, right. Nothing at all." It's just not fair, I thought. Leslie has to do the same project I do, but she isn't working half as hard. She's too busy flirting with Dave.

When I got home that day, I lay facedown on my bed. I couldn't get my mind off Dave. I tried to work on my project, but I couldn't concentrate. I just wanted it to be finished.

The next day I headed off to the library again at lunch. This was it. I was going to read over the final draft of my report and hand it in to Mrs. Blume tomorrow. I sat down in the back of the room and took it out of my backpack.

"You'll find a whole assortment of short stories in this section," the librarian said behind me.

"Thanks," said a familiar male voice. I glanced up. It was Dave! I quickly turned back to my paper. My heart was racing. I turned the pages of my report, frantically trying to look busy. I could hear him shuffling around behind me.

Then he walked toward my table. I didn't know what to do. Should I look up or not? I wondered. I looked up. He smiled at me as he walked by.

"Hi," I said. I can't believe I said that, I thought.

"Hi," he said, sitting down at the table next to mine. I'm coming to the library every day for the rest of the year, I thought. He opened a book and started reading. I looked back down at my paper.

The rest of the period flew by. When the bell rang, Dave and I got up at the same time.

"Have you gotten hit by any footballs lately?" he asked.

I laughed. "No, not lately." He remembers me, I thought. I can't believe it!

We walked out the door together. "See ya," he said.

"Bye." I couldn't stop smiling as I rushed to my next class. I couldn't wait to tell Pam what happened.

"Blue Eyes talked to me! He really talked to me!" I blurted out when we met after school.

"Where did you see him? What did he say? What did you do?" she asked all in one breath. I told her everything.

The next day Pam came over after school. I had handed in my project in the morning, and I had a permanent smile on my face.

"I'm done!" I sang, dancing around the living room. My mom laughed.

"She's been bouncing off walls all day," Pam said.

"How about going out to dinner to celebrate?" asked my mom. "You can come too, Pam."

"I'll watch Timmy while you guys go out to dinner," offered Darlene.

"Thanks," I said.

So off we went to my favorite Mexican restaurant, Chili Willy's. I had been craving nachos for weeks. The hostess seated us at a table in the middle of the room.

"Ooh! Look at him!" Pam whispered to me as a tall boy with sandy-blond hair walked over. The boy filled our water glasses and left.

"Smile at him," she said, nudging me. "Remember the book!"

"What are you two troublemakers whispering about?" asked my mom.

"Nothing, Mom. Honest," I said. Pam giggled.

The boy passed our table again. Pam smiled at him. He smiled back. It was working!

"Excuse me," my mom said to the boy. He stopped and walked over to our table. Pam's whole face turned bright red. "May we have some chips and salsa?"

"Sure," he said, and glanced at Pam. She was staring at the table.

Mom turned to Pam with a knowing grin. "Nothing, huh?"

Every time our busboy passed our table, he smiled

at Pam. "More water?" he asked her one time. Her glass was practically full.

"Sure," Pam said, with a half-smile.

I leaned over to her. "You're blushing," I teased.

"I am not."

As we were leaving the restaurant, our busboy walked toward us. "See ya," he said. I thought Pam was going to faint.

When we got outside, she was all smiles. "He talked to me," Pam babbled. "Did you see how he looked at me?" She put her hand on her heart and threw her head back dramatically. "My future husband!"

My mom and I looked at each other and laughed. We drove to Pam's house and dropped her off. "See you tomorrow," she said. "And don't forget the book. It's time to get back to business."

The next day at school Pam and I reviewed our book. "It's a good start," she said. "But we need much, much more."

When I arrived home from school, there was a letter from Cathy waiting for me.

Hey, Marci,

You gave me a great idea for my communications paper: I've decided to write about cross-gender interfacing—in other words, flirting!

I interviewed twenty-five college freshmen

*to see how they flirted. Most of the answers
were pretty interesting. I've also been watching a lot of people and writing down my ob-
servations. The first section of my paper is
on nonverbal flirting. Here are some ideas
based on my research. Good luck!*

1. Get the person you're interested in to
notice you. Some of the girls I spoke to said
to be loud so that the guy will notice you.
Others said to act helpless so that he can of-
fer to help. For example, one girl said she
met her boyfriend when she fell off her bike
and he helped her up.
    A few girls said that acting dizzy (meaning
dumb) works too.
    Personally, I wouldn't try any of these
methods. I think they're way too fake, and I
can't believe anyone would act like that. I
certainly couldn't see you and Pam trying to
act helpless and dumb.
    So my basic advice is, just be yourself.
Your main hurdle will be getting over your
fear of boys, but I know you can do it, and I
think the rest of my suggestions might help
in that department.
    2. Let the guy know you are interested. If
he doesn't know you're interested, you probably won't meet him. Here are some ways to
show him:

—look directly at him;
—when you make eye contact, hold your stare a few seconds longer than usual;
—smile at him.

3. *Make yourself available.* Don't spend all your time with a group of people or even one girlfriend. You are more approachable if you're alone. Sit by yourself sometimes. Or take a walk. I know this sounds difficult, but think about it this way—you wouldn't walk up to a group of guys, would you? Well, most guys wouldn't walk up to a group of girls either.

If you're alone, don't make yourself look too busy. Otherwise guys won't want to interrupt you. The girls I spoke to swear this is true.

4. *Don't overdress.* If you dress up too much, you will look intimidating. Dress casually and you'll be easier to approach. You'll also be more comfortable, so you'll look and feel more relaxed.

5. Once you get the guy's attention and are talking to him, there are a few things to keep in mind. Nine of the girls I interviewed said that you should keep eye contact while you are talking to the guy. Don't look around, or you'll seem uninterested.

Also, you'll get better results if you position your body toward your subject. If you *cross your legs, cross them toward the person, not away. The same thing is true of the way you place your body. Turn toward your subject to face him. If you turn your body away, it looks as if you are trying to get away.*

I think that's enough to get you started. The second part of my paper will be on verbal flirting, and how to keep a conversation going once you meet the right person. I'll keep you posted.

And remember, I'm six years older than you and still don't know how to flirt as well as I'd like. So, don't worry. You'll develop your own style. Just give yourself time.

I hope all is well. Give a kiss to your whole family for me.

> *Love,*
> *Cathy*

I ran into my mom's room and dialed Pam's number.

"Guess what I got in the mail!" I said when she answered the phone. "A letter from Cathy. It explains everything!"

"I'm on my way!" Pam hung up.

When she came over, we sat down and copied everything from the letter into our book.

"Stand alone? Is she crazy?" Pam said. "We can't do that! It'll look like we have no friends."

"I know, but think about it. When I met Dave, I was alone. I was waiting for you," I said.

"Maybe you're right," Pam said, "but we'll need to practice this."

"How about Saturday?" I suggested.

"You're on."

When Saturday finally arrived, Pam and I were ready. We were going to the mall across town to practice our flirting.

"Do I look all right?" Pam asked. She was wearing her faded jeans and a bright-aqua shirt.

"You look great." I had on my baggy black pants and a light green shirt. I was definitely comfortable, just as Cathy had advised. No more makeup or sexy clothes for us.

My mom drove us to the mall at noon. "I'll pick you up at four," she said. "Have fun shopping, girls."

We wandered inside. Pam nudged me. "Look," she said, pointing at two guys sitting on a bench. "Let's start with them."

My stomach flip-flopped. Couldn't we wait another two minutes? I wondered anxiously.

"We'll go stand over there," said Pam. I followed her. Neither of us looked at the guys as we passed, but Pam stopped near them. I felt really stupid.

"Okay, now we have to let them know we're interested," she said. "Let's look at them."

"Okay," I said. I don't like this, I thought.

"Ready? One, two, three—look." I turned toward the guys. They were looking right at us. Oh, God! I thought. This is so embarrassing!

I caught the brown-haired boy's eye. He smiled. I looked away. Pam laughed. "It worked!" she said.

"Shhh!" I said, "They'll know we're talking about them."

"That's the whole point," Pam said. She looked at them again. I peeked out of the corner of my eye. This time Pam smiled. They both smiled back. "This is kind of fun," she said.

"Pammy! How are you? And Marci!" a voice came from behind us. It was Pam's Aunt Maggie. She hugged Pam. "It's so nice to see you! What are you doing at this end of town?"

"Shopping," Pam said. "How are you?" While her aunt asked her about school, and her family, and her summer vacation, the boys got up, looked over and smiled at us, and left.

"Well, it was great to see you too," Pam called when Aunt Maggie finally said good-bye.

We looked at each other and then over where the boys had been sitting. "What awful timing!" Pam grumbled. "Well, I guess it's on to our next subjects."

"It was a good start, though," I said. "They really did smile at us. Let's try it again."

"*That's* what I like to hear. Come on!" Pam pulled me toward the food section. "Let's get some frozen yogurt. I'm starving."

We walked over to the stand. The guy behind the counter wasn't much older than we were. Pam smiled at him. He smiled back.

"What can I get you?" he asked.

"I'll have a small chocolate with carob chips and cookie crumbs," Pam said.

"And I'll have a small half chocolate and half vanilla with cookie crumbs," I added.

"Coming right up." He served us two dishes overflowing with yogurt.

"Geez!" Pam said. "Those are huge."

"It's a special size just for you," the guy said, smiling.

"Thanks," I said, smiling back.

"Bye!" Pam said.

We sat down at a table on the other side. "Can you believe it?" Pam said. "That was so nice."

"No kidding."

"Look," Pam said. Three young guys walked by and sat down at a table near us.

"Here we go again," I said.

"Practice makes perfect," said Pam. She glanced in their direction and nudged me. "Look at them," she said. "And look friendly."

I looked at them. One of the guys was staring

right at me. I dropped my eyes. Pam smiled. One of the guys smiled back. This sure does work, I thought, watching them both.

"Should we separate and try sitting alone?" Pam said.

"No way!" I yelped.

"But this is supposed to be our practice time."

"Well, if *you* want to try it alone, *I'll* go to the bathroom."

"I don't know." Now Pam was undecided.

"Okay, I'm going now. I'll be right back." I got up.

"Marci!" Pam began. But it was too late. I walked through the food section, around the corner and into the bathroom. I looked in the mirror and fixed my hair. After a few minutes I went back out and walked toward our table.

I stopped short. The three guys were sitting at our table! I wasn't sure I wanted to go back to my seat, but finally I walked over. One of the guys jumped up. "I took your place. I'm sorry." He motioned for me to sit down. I didn't know what to do.

"Marci, this is Bob and Tom and Billy," Pam said smoothly.

"Hi," I said.

"Do you two go to school together?" Bob asked. His green eyes stared right into mine.

"Yes," I replied airily. "We've known each other forever."

"Same here," said Billy. His brown hair flopped over his eyes. "Our parents were friends before we were even born."

"Really?" Pam said. "That's a long time."

"Tommy!" a voice called. We turned around. An older woman was walking over. "Are you kids ready?"

Tommy blushed. He looked down. "Okay, Mom. We'll be right there." She left. He turned back to us. "Mothers! Sometimes they can be such a pain."

The boys all got up. "Bye," Bob said.

"Maybe we'll see you around," said Billy. They left.

"As soon as you left they just came over and asked me my name," Pam said with a grin. "I almost said Danielle, but I resisted. Could you die?"

We wandered around for the next hour until we met my mom. Nothing much happened after the three boys, but we certainly were more daring. Pam even smiled at an older cute guy. He said hi.

When we got to my house, we ran up to my room and I wrote down everything in our book.

FLIRTING EXPEDITION #2: THE MALL

IT WORKED! CATHY WAS RIGHT. EVERY TIME WE SMILED AT A GUY, HE SMILED BACK. THE FROZEN-YOGURT GUY EVEN GAVE US EXTRA-BIG SERVINGS AFTER WE SMILED AT HIM. AND WHEN

PAM SAT ALONE, THREE GUYS CAME RIGHT
OVER. IT WAS UNBELIEVABLE! AND KIND OF
FUN. WE'RE GOING TO TRY THIS IN SCHOOL
ON MONDAY.

Monday was wonderful—especially now that my project was finished and I didn't have to go to the library at lunch. Instead, I sat down in the sun, closed my eyes and enjoyed its warmth on my skin while I waited for Pam.

"Hey, wake up!" Pam said as she walked over. "Today's the day."

"What day?"

"Our first school flirting test," she said. "Remember?"

"Here?" I said. The bottom of my stomach suddenly dropped out. "Oh, I don't know, Pam. Maybe I'm not ready for this."

"Come on! Look for likely subjects."

Oh, God, I thought, reluctantly following Pam toward the lunch lines. Here we go again. I looked around me. There were familiar faces everywhere.

"It was easier across town with people we didn't

know," I said. "We can't do it here. What if some-one we know sees us in action?"

"Oh, come on. Don't be chicken," said Pam. "We'll find people we don't know."

"This line is the shortest," I said, trying to change the subject. We got in line.

"Look!" Pam said. "Those guys are watching us." She nodded in the direction of two guys standing a few lines away.

"They look kind of familiar."

"Oh, you're just paranoid. I've never seen them before in my life," she said. "Let's practice on them. You first."

"No way—this is *your* idea. You go first."

"Okay. Let's look at them at the same time," Pam said. "And remember, hold your stare longer than usual."

My heart was pounding. I peeked behind us to see if anyone was watching. All clear.

"Ready?" Pam said.

"No."

"Marci!"

"Okay."

"One, two, three," Pam counted. "Now!" We both looked over at the same time. The two guys were talking to each other.

Phew, I thought. I'm saved. But suddenly they both looked right at us. I didn't know what to do. Pam nudged me. She smiled. The brown-haired boy looked behind him and then back at us. I looked at the ground.

Pam smiled again. I couldn't believe it—he was smiling back! The other one, the one with blond hair, smiled too.

So did I.

"Can I help you?" a woman yelled. I realized we were standing at the end of an empty line.

I rushed up to the window. "Sorry," I said, blushing.

"Two turkey combos and two Diet Cokes," said Pam.

I looked around. I was sure everybody was staring at us. We got our food and headed back to our table without looking anywhere near where the boys were standing.

"I don't know, Pam," I said when we had sat down. "Maybe we need to practice more."

"Practice what?" a male voice asked. I jumped. It was the two guys from the line.

"Piano," Pam said quickly. "We're in a recital."

I kept staring at the two guys. Where do I know them from? I wondered.

"The car!" the brown-haired boy yelled.

"That's it!" the blond said.

"What are you talking about?" I asked.

"Aren't you the girls who live in a car?"

Oh no! It was the car-wash guys! I looked at Pam. Suddenly we both cracked up.

"And you're our maids," Pam said.

The guys laughed. "At your service," the blond said, bowing.

"Do you mind if we sit down?" the other one asked. "These trays are getting heavy."

"No, go right ahead," Pam said.

"I didn't know you girls went to school here," the blond said.

"Yup, we do," Pam said. I felt as if my mouth had been wired shut. I couldn't think of anything to say.

"I'm Jeff," the brown-haired one said.

"And I'm Jeff too," the blond said.

"Just call us Jeff One and Jeff Two," the brown-haired boy said. "I'm Jeff One."

"No, I'm Jeff One," the blond said.

Pam and I laughed. "This could get very confusing," she said.

"Okay, he can be Jeff One," said the blond. "Now, what are your names?"

Tiffany, I thought. "I'm Pam," Pam said. "And this is Pam too."

"No way," Jeff One said. "That would be too cute. Pam and Pam and Jeff and Jeff. And we could name our kids Pam and Jeff."

"No, I'm kidding," Pam said. "I *am* Pam, but this is Marci."

"Well, nice to meet you, Pam and Marci," said Jeff Two.

We smiled. The boys started eating their lunch. I took a bite out of my sandwich. I looked at Pam. No one said anything.

I hate long silences, I thought. Why can't I think of something to say? I opened my potato chips and started nibbling on one nervously.

"What grade are you girls in?" said Jeff One.

I tried to swallow my mouthful as fast as I could. I practically choked on it. "Seventh," I finally managed.

"Ooh, young ones," said Jeff Two.

"And what grade are you in?" Pam asked. I could tell she was slightly annoyed.

"We're in ninth grade," Jeff One said.

"Ooh, old ones," said Pam.

"She's pretty feisty," Jeff Two said.

"I guess that's what happens when you grow up in a car," Jeff One said.

"It's a tough life on the road," Pam told him.

I tried to think of something to say. My mind was a total blank.

"What time do you work today?" Jeff One asked Jeff Two.

"Four," Jeff Two said.

"So, what's your next class?" Pam asked me. She knew my schedule perfectly, but we had to talk about something!

"Math," I said. I ate another potato chip.

"Well, girls, we've got to head up to our soccer meeting," Jeff One said. "See ya around."

"Bye," Jeff Two said as they got up.

We waved. "Bye," Pam said.

"I didn't think we'd have to talk to them," I said when they were gone.

"I know," Pam said. "That was kind of scary."

"I can't believe it was the car-wash guys! I thought I'd faint!"

"At least our flirt worked," Pam said.

"Except we still don't know how to carry on a conversation," I said. "I didn't have a thing to say."

"Me neither. They asked all the questions."

"Maybe when we flirt, we should just smile and run away," I suggested.

"Look, there's Peter Johnson!" said Pam.

I froze. "Who's he with?" I was afraid to look over.

"I can't tell," she said. "Wait! I think it's Blue Eyes."

I glanced out of the corner of my eye. It *was* Blue Eyes.

"Should we try flirting with them?" Pam said. "It's been working with everyone else."

"Are you crazy?" I squeaked. "I couldn't!"

"I'm going to look over," Pam said. She looked at me. "Really, I am."

I laughed. "Okay, Pam. Go right ahead."

"I can't." She sighed.

"I can't either."

"Let's look at them now, together."

"No way!"

"Uh-oh." Pam grabbed my arm.

"What? What?"

"They're coming toward us."

"You're kidding."

"I am not."

I glanced over. "Oh no! You're right!"

"Still?" Pam asked.

"What do we do?"

It was too late.

"Hi, Pam. Hi, Marci," Peter said.

"Oh, hi, Peter," Pam said. I just smiled. I couldn't open my mouth.

I looked up and caught Dave's eye. I quickly looked down. He's so cute! I thought.

"You know Dave, don't you?" Peter said.

"Sort of," I said, trying to stay calm. Dave smiled. I thought I was going to die.

"I don't," Pam said. "Nice to meet you."

"You too," said Dave.

"I'm having a Halloween party," Peter told us. "Here. I hope you guys can come." He handed each of us an envelope.

"Thanks," Pam said.

"Sure." Peter nodded. "We'll see ya later."

"Bye," I got out.

"Bye," said Dave. They walked away. My heart was thudding.

"Keep talking," Pam said under her breath. "Pretend it's no big deal."

"Big deal?" I squeaked. "Are you kidding? The

two best-looking guys in the whole school, possibly even our future husbands, just came over and invited us to the party of the year. What makes you think that it's a big deal?"

"Are they gone?" Pam asked.

I looked behind me just as they disappeared around the corner of a building.

"They're gone," I said. Pam ripped open her envelope.

Inside was a mimeographed sheet of blue paper, with pictures of ghosts and pumpkins all over it.

IT'S A DAY-AFTER-HALLOWEEN PARTY!
AND YOU'RE INVITED!

WHEN: November 1, 7:00 p.m.

WHERE: Peter's house
2633 Cordelia Rd.

WHY: Why not?

DRESS: Haunting attire!

"Can you believe it?" I asked.

"Hardly," said Pam. "I wonder who else is invited."

"I don't care, as long as I get to talk to Dave."

Leslie suddenly walked around the corner. "Hi, girls!" she called. She was holding an invitation in her hand. "Oh, good, were you invited too?" she said. "Isn't this going to be great? What are we going to wear?"

"I want to be a devil," Pam announced the next day at lunch.

"And I could be an angel," I said.

"Well, what about me?" Leslie interjected. "We said we're doing this *together*."

Pam rolled her eyes at me. Pam and I had wanted to dress as a pair, but Leslie had asked if she could join us. Not wanting to hurt her, we agreed.

"I've got it!" Pam said, grinning wickedly. "Let's be cavewomen! We can carry clubs and clobber the boys when they get out of hand!"

"That's great!" Leslie said. "A clan of cave-women."

"I like it!" I said. "Ooga booga."

For the next week we ran around gathering stuff for our costumes. Leslie bought shaggy gray material, Pam bought plastic clubs and I got gray furry slippers and three big plastic dog bones to put in our hair.

We worked on the costumes at Leslie's house. Her mom loved to sew, and she helped us piece the costumes together. "Dave is going to love this," Leslie announced one day, holding her costume up in front of her.

My body tensed right up. Pam glanced at me. Why does she always have to talk about him? I thought. I felt really uncomfortable every time Leslie mentioned Dave's name. Pam thought I should tell Leslie that I liked him too, but I didn't want to. After all, she knew him much better than I did. Even though I hadn't told her that I had a crush on him, I couldn't help thinking that she talked about him just to make me jealous. Leslie seemed to have radar for these kinds of things. I tried to ignore her until my mom picked us up later that afternoon.

"How are the costumes coming?" my mom asked when we got in the car.

"Great!" Pam said. "But we still have some work to do on them."

"Well, you've got two more weeks," my mom said. "Oh, Marci, a letter came from Cathy today. She wrote 'the final chapter' on the envelope. What does that mean?"

"I don't know," I said as casually as possible. I tried not to smile. Pam and I looked at each other, eyes gleaming. This was what we'd been waiting for. "Can Pam stay for dinner tonight, Mom?" I asked.

"Of course she can," my mom said. "But we're only having leftovers."

"That's fine by me," Pam said. "Thanks!"

At long last, I thought, we're going to learn how to talk to boys!

When my mom stopped the car, Pam and I jumped out and ran into the house. The letter was sitting on the kitchen counter.

We grabbed it and ran upstairs to my room. "Now we're really going to be prepared for Peter's party," said Pam. "Open it! Open it!" I tore the envelope open and pulled out the letter.

Hi, Marci,

Are you ready for the second part of my communications paper, Conversational Skills?

My research for this section was pretty extensive. I read a lot, and I did dozens of personal interviews. I'll just tell you the things that I think you'll be most interested in.

By the way, write me back and let me know how things are going—I'd like to know if these suggestions help. Besides, you owe me a letter.

Basically, I've tried to focus on things that might work for you when you're talking to a guy you like. But many of these ideas will work for meeting or talking to anyone, male or female.

Just remember: Starting and carrying on a conversation can be very difficult for all of us, young or old—especially with someone we have a crush on.

1. *Asking questions.*

The type of question that you ask is very important. You want to stir up as much conversation as possible. The books that I read suggest avoiding closed-ended questions, which elicit only a short reply.

Here are some examples of closed-ended questions:

> *"Where do you live?"*
> *"Isn't this class hard?"*
> *"Do you play football?"*

If you want to learn facts about someone, this type of question is great. But if you want to carry on a conversation, they'll lead to a dead end.

Try open-ended questions instead. They'll promote longer answers. Or if you do begin your conversation with a closed-ended question, just follow it with an open-ended one. This will show that you are interested in the person.

Here are some open-ended questions:

"How do you like living on top of a canyon?"

"In what way do you find this class to be difficult?"

"How did you get involved with playing football on this team?"

One advantage to asking questions is that you can control the conversation and talk about something you're interested in. In other words, something that you know about.

Another tip is to prepare questions in advance. I'm sure you have someone in mind right now who you would love to talk to, right? Well, find out a little bit about him and study up.

For example, if he's interested in football or soccer, you might want to do a bit of research. (Ask your dad about football. I know he loves it.) You'll really impress the guy with your knowledge—even if you don't know much, you'll know what questions to ask. The possibilities are endless. You can find out what he is studying in school, what his outside interests are, etc., etc.

2. Compliments.

Everyone likes to get compliments, so use them. Comment on a shirt, a project or a

hairstyle that you like—but don't lie. Choose
something you really do like. On the other
hand, don't overdo it. If you compliment
someone too frequently, it can make you
seem insincere.

3. *Listening.*

    It's important to listen well, for a lot of
reasons. It encourages the person to continue
talking, and it gives you a chance to really
understand what he or she is saying.

    And Marci, don't get flustered if he's cute.
Just pay attention to what he says and you'll
probably think of something to say next.
You can always ask another question—pref-
erably an open-ended one!

4. *Starting a conversation.*

    Like I said before, starting a conversation
with a stranger or someone you don't know
very well is difficult. (Especially if you have a
crush on him.)

    You've got a few basic topics to choose
from when you start a conversation. There is
the situation, the other person and yourself.
The easiest approach is to talk about your
situation, which is what you have in com-
mon.

    There are three ways to begin the conver-
sation: You can ask a question, voice an

opinion or state a fact. It all depends on which is easiest for you to do.

If the guy is in your class, ask him how long it took him to do his project or why he chose a certain book to read. If you're standing outside, you could just say, "It sure is a gorgeous day." Or if you're waiting in line for lunch say, "This line sure is long today."

I know these remarks sound kind of stupid, but they will break the ice. A smile following his reaction always helps too.

Well, Marci, there you have it. I think that gives you plenty of information. Now, go out and start talking! What's his name, anyway?

Don't worry if it's hard at first. It takes practice! And remember, there are plenty of adults who still have problems with this stuff.

Good luck and write soon. Say hi to Pam for me.

Love,
Cathy

"Wow!" Pam said. "That's a lot of stuff."

"No kidding," I agreed. "I didn't know people actually wrote books on things like this."

"We're going to have to really study this part," Pam said. "And practice a lot."

"I'll write it all down later tonight," I said. "Should I bring the book to school tomorrow for reference?"

"Don't go out without it," said Pam.

At lunch the next day Pam and I read over Cathy's letter from our book—I'd copied it down word for word the night before.

"We have to learn about football," said Pam. "Peter and Dave both play."

"Good idea," I said. "I'll ask my dad about it tomorrow."

"And I'll talk to my mom tonight. She loves football," Pam said.

Then we practiced asking closed-ended and open-ended questions. "Why do you find Dave so attractive?" Pam asked.

"Because he has the most beautiful blue eyes I've ever seen, and I'm going to marry him," I said dreamily.

"How do you plan to do that?"

"First I will talk to him at Peter's party, and then he will ask me on a date, and before you know it, we'll be married." We laughed.

"Now ask me something," said Pam.

"Well, Pamela, in what way do you feel that your Halloween costume will help you to talk to Peter?"

"Ooga booga," said Pam. "Me girl, him boy. He not talk to me, I hit him with club."

"And how do you feel hitting him with the club will solve this problem?"

"If he doesn't talk to me, at least he won't be able to talk to anyone else."

"This is great." I laughed. "We're going to be pros by party time."

"And Leslie won't have a chance with Dave," Pam said. "By then you'll know all about football and soccer. What does she know about those things anyway?"

"Absolutely nothing," I replied.

After school my mom picked me up. Pam had a doctor's appointment, so we had to put our conversational skills on hold until later.

"C'mere, Marci!" Timmy said when I got home. "Look what I made in school!" He held up a collage made of leaves and twigs. "I want you to have it."

"Thanks, pal," I said. Timmy really was a cute kid, even though he could be a pain sometimes. I put my backpack down and gave him a hug. "Will you sign it for me? Then when you're famous, I'll have your autograph." I took a couple of books from my pack, digging through everything until I found a pencil. I gave it to him.

"Here goes," he said, scribbling his name across the collage.

"Thanks, champ!" I said, and kissed him. I was putting everything back in my pack when my mother called.

"Marci, can you help me in the kitchen?"

I ended up chopping mushrooms and onions for the next hour. My mom was making one of my favorite pasta dishes—linguini with mushroom cream sauce. I ate so much at dinner that I couldn't move. I just managed to roll myself upstairs and do a little English homework before I went to sleep.

The next morning I was wide awake at six. I took a shower and put on my turquoise pants and a bright pink shirt. I was in a colorful mood.

Maybe I'll practice questions on someone today, I mused. Now, what was it that Cathy said about open-ended questions?

I opened my pack to get out the flirting book. It wasn't there. I dumped everything out on my bed. I found all my books for science, social studies and English. But no flirting book.

I looked in the pack again. Nothing. I threw everything back in. I looked under my bed, in my closet, on my floor.

This can't be happening, I thought. I ran downstairs. I looked in the kitchen. Nothing. Horrible thoughts raced through my mind. Had I left it on the lunch table? What if Peter and Dave picked it up by mistake? If anyone found it, I would die! I dialed Pam's number.

"Do you have our book?" I asked frantically.

"No, you do," she said. "Don't you?"

"Meet me at the bus stop, pronto!" I said, and hung up. Where could it be? I ran upstairs and checked my room again. Nothing.

"Bye, Mom!" I yelled as I rushed out the door. What would happen if someone found it? I didn't even want to think about it. It had names and dates—everything! I ran faster and faster.

Pam was already at the bus stop when I got there. She was out of breath from running.

"What happened?"

"I don't know," I said. "It just disappeared!"

"Things don't just disappear," she said. "Did you put it in your pack after lunch yesterday?"

"I think so. I mean, I thought so," I said. I couldn't remember anymore.

As soon as we got to school, Pam and I ran to the lunch area. We searched everywhere, including the lost and found. Our book wasn't there.

"We're ruined," said Pam.

"It will turn up. It has to," I said.

"Yeah, probably in Jerome's hands," Pam moaned. I cringed at the thought.

Jerome sat right behind me in social studies. "So, what's new, Marci?" he asked. He never talked to me in class unless he had something to tease me about. And he had a horrible smirk on his face. He has the book. I'm sure of it! I thought.

"Nothing," I answered, without turning around.

"Nothing?" He leaned toward me. "You're awfully quiet today."

Now I was convinced he had it and was just tormenting me. Stay calm, I told myself. "I feel like being quiet," I said, twirling my hair nervously around my finger.

Luckily our teacher walked in the room, and Jerome didn't say another word to me. Class seemed to go on for hours. As soon as the bell rang I ran out the door.

At lunch Pam and I sat at our usual table. We wanted to hide, but that would have been too obvious.

"This is just awful!" said Pam after I told her what had happened in social studies.

"What do we do?" I asked urgently.

"Oh *nooo*," she moaned.

"What's the matter now?"

"It's the boys. They're all together," she said. "I just *know* they're talking about us. Now they're laughing. What do we do?"

"Hide."

"It's too late. Here they come."

I wanted to crawl under the table. I could hear Jerome's horrible laugh. It was getting louder and louder.

"Hi, girls!" Jerome said.

"Hi," I said without looking up. They kept walking.

"Why didn't they say anything?" I whispered to Pam.

"They're tormenting us," Pam said. "They just want to see us squirm."

"Well, we're squirming."

The rest of the day crawled by. I sat on the opposite side of the room from Peter Johnson in science, and I couldn't wait for it to end.

My mom wasn't picking us up because Darlene needed the car. Of all days to have to take the bus! What a nightmare!

We sat in the last seat all the way in the back and barely said a word. It was definitely low-profile time.

"We could switch schools," Pam suggested as the bus started.

"Or wear masks," I said.

"Hi there," Jerome said, getting out of his seat and sitting down directly in front of us. "How's school treating you?"

"Just fine, thanks," Pam said.

"Well, good," he said with a horrible smirk. "A bit different from last year, huh? You've really got to stay on top of those books."

"Yeah," I said, wishing he'd face the front of the bus instead of us. We finally arrived at our stop.

"Bye, girls," Jerome said loudly when we got off.

"That's it! He's got to have it," Pam said. "Did you hear what he said about books? I'm going to go home and hibernate."

"I'll call you later," I said.

"Marci! Marci!" Timmy yelled when I walked in the door. I ignored him. "Come look, Marci!"

What a pest he could be! I walked into the kitchen, opened the refrigerator and took out some bread, turkey, lettuce, tomato and mayonnaise. I could always eat my life away, I thought as I piled everything onto the bread.

"Marci!" Timmy called.

"What?" I yelled back, cutting the sandwich in half.

"Come look."

I stomped into the den. My life is practically over, I thought, and I have to deliver a critical analysis of a five-year-old's artwork.

"It's a puppy," he said, holding up a brown-and-blue picture. "Mommy said we might be able to get one, so I drew the kind I want."

"That's lovely, Timmy. Just lovely."

"Look at this one!" He held up another drawing. This dog had yellow and red spots. It looked diseased.

"It's very nice," I said.

Suddenly I noticed something in his lap. "What's that?" I gasped.

"Nothing," he said. "Just my drawing board."

I reached down and grabbed it. My book! My flirting book! I didn't know whether to kiss him or hit him.

"Where did you get this?" I yelled.

"I found it on the floor," he said. "I was using it to draw on."

"Oh, brother!" I took the book and ran upstairs. I flipped through the pages. It was all there, safe in my hands! Clutching it tightly, I ran into my mom's room and dialed Pam's number.

"I can't believe it!" she yelled when I told her what happened. "We're saved!"

"We won't have to wear masks," I said.

"And we can go to the party." Pam sighed. "I'm so happy."

"Well, call me later," I said.

"Okay. Bye." Pam hung up.

The phone rang. I picked it up. "Hello?" I said cheerfully.

"Hi, Marci!" said my dad. "How's my big fisherwoman doing?"

"Great, Dad. Just super. I'm glad you called. Will you teach me all about football?"

"Football? Why? Are you taking up the sport?"

"No, I just need to know."

"Okay. I'll tell you all about it in a minute. But first I have some great news."

"What?" I asked.

"Well, the fishing trip is all set. We set sail on November 1."

My heart dropped. It couldn't be. November 1 was Peter's party. How could this be happening to me?

"Great, Dad," I muttered. "Listen, I've got to go. Bye." I hung up just in time. Tears rolled down my cheeks. It just couldn't be true.

I dialed Pam's number. I could barely speak. "Pam," I managed to blurt out.

"What's wrong?"

"I can't go," I sobbed.

"Go where?" Pam said.

I couldn't talk. I tried to take a deep breath.

"Take it easy, Marci. I'll be right over," Pam said, and hung up. I ran into my room and shut the door. I couldn't control myself. Why have I been practicing how to flirt? I thought. It was all for nothing. I threw the flirting book across the room. Now Leslie was going to get Dave. I just knew it.

I won't go fishing, I thought. It just isn't fair. Dad can't ask me to ruin my life.

Pam came bounding through my door. "What's wrong? What happened?"

She gasped when I told her.

Tears were pouring down my face. "I'm going to the party," I sobbed. "My dad should have told me earlier."

"Of course he should have," Pam said. "After all our work on flirting and the costumes! Oh, Marci, you just have to go to the party. I don't want to go without you."

"I'll just call my dad and tell him I can't go," I said.

Just then my mom walked into my room. I told her what had happened. "It's your choice, Marci," she said when I was through. "You don't have to go with your father. I'm sure he'll understand."

"I wouldn't go," Darlene said when she heard. "And miss a good party? No way."

Pam left a few minutes later. She had to be home for dinner. I skipped mine. I just wasn't hungry. Then my dad called back. I made Darlene say I wasn't home. I lay on my bed with my head pressed into my pillow.

I knew my dad had been counting on this trip. He's going to be crushed, I thought. But so am I.

I picked up my flirting book and held it in my hands. All that work for nothing, I thought. This'll be my only chance with Dave—if Leslie has her way.

I was so confused. Then I thought of Cathy. She always knew what to do. I went into my mom's room and dialed Cathy's number.

"Hi, stranger!" she said when she heard my voice. "How's the flirting going?"

It felt good to hear her voice after so long. I told

her everything. I read her some stuff from our book and told her about the mall, the missing book and Dave.

"You're doing great!" She laughed. "You'll be a pro before you know it. And listen, I got an *A* on my report, thanks to your idea."

Then I told her about my dad and the fishing trip and the party. She was silent for a moment. "Oh, Marci, that's tough," she said. "I know how much the party means to you. Dave will be there, won't he?"

"Yes," I said. I felt the tears welling in my eyes. "What do I do now?"

"Well, you have to think of your father, too," she said. "He didn't pick that date on purpose. He didn't know about your party. And the trip means so much to him."

"I know."

"He never gets to see you," she went on. "And you've been going on this trip for years."

"I know," I said through my tears. "But I want to go to Peter's party so badly. Everyone will be there. And if I'm not there, Leslie will snag Dave for sure."

"Well, Marci, you just have to weigh your priorities. I know going to this party seems like a life-or-death situation to you, but the fishing trip is just as important to your father."

We talked for a few more minutes and then hung up. I thought about Dave and his beautiful blue eyes, and Leslie and her horrible crush. I thought about my dad and how hurt he would be if I didn't go with him.

I dialed my father's number. I still had no idea what I was going to say. "Hi, Dad," I said.

"Honey, are you all right? You hung up so fast. Is something wrong?"

"No, I'm fine. I just had to go; someone was at the door."

"Oh, I was worried about you."

"I'm fine, Dad."

"So, what do you think? Are we going to win the fishing contest again?"

I took a deep breath. "Sure, Dad. You bet."

12

The next few weeks were really hard. Leslie and Pam were finishing up their costumes, and all they talked about was the party.

"Too bad you can't make it," Leslie said. "It's going to be great. Everyone's going."

"Right," I said. I had a lump in my throat. "I'm sure it will be wonderful."

On Halloween night Pam and I took Timmy trick or treating around the neighborhood. Timmy was dressed as a pirate and kept wanting to fight with his cardboard sword. Pam and I wore our cavewoman outfits just for fun. None of our friends from school were out in costume because Peter's party was the next night and everyone was going there.

At least I'm getting some use out of this outfit, I thought as we walked down the street. Even if no one sees it except little kids.

"I'll keep tabs on Leslie," Pam promised on the

way home. "Don't worry, I won't even let her talk to Dave."

"Thanks," I said. There were tears in my eyes. "Good luck. Here's the book. You can do some last-minute reviewing." I certainly don't need it now, I thought.

I woke up at seven-thirty the next morning. My dad was picking me up at eight, but I didn't need to do much. After all, I was just going to be hanging out on a boat with a bunch of fish.

I put on my jeans and an old oversized T-shirt. I put another pair of pants, a sweatshirt and a flannel shirt in my duffel bag, along with my toothbrush and hairbrush. Then I grabbed my windbreaker and tied it around my shoulders, picked up my fishing pole, and carried everything downstairs.

At five after eight my dad arrived. "I brought you something," he said. He pulled a bright red baseball cap from behind his back. On the crown it said #1 FISHERWOMAN.

I smiled. "Thanks, Dad," I said. I put the cap on.

I ran upstairs to say good-bye to my mom while Dad put my stuff in the car. Timmy came charging down the stairs. "Daddy, Daddy!" he shouted. Dad picked him up and threw him in the air.

"How's my sport today?" he said.

"Great, Dad. Catch a lot of fish."

"We're sure gonna try," he said.

"Bye, Timmy," I called, and we headed out the door.

The dock was about a forty-minute drive from my house and the boat was scheduled to leave at nine-thirty.

"How's school?" my dad asked.

"Great," I said. "I got an *A* on my project in social studies."

"Honey, that's wonderful! Congratulations." He reached over and squeezed my hand.

I was pretty proud of myself too. I had worked really hard on the project. And Mrs. Blume even hung my map at the front of the room.

When we were about halfway to the dock, we ran into a major traffic jam. Cars were backed up for miles. I tensed up, waiting for my dad to blow up like he always did in traffic.

"There must have been an accident around here," he said. "Oh, well, that'll give us more time to talk before we have to be social."

I looked at him in amazement. Was this my dad? Smiling in a traffic jam? It couldn't be.

"So, do you have any big crushes in school?" he asked. I still couldn't believe how calm he was.

"No, not really," I said. That was the last thing that I wanted to talk about.

"I remember when I was your age," my dad said. "There was this blond girl named Mary Pat that I had the biggest crush on."

I couldn't help smiling. My dad had never told me things like this before.

"She lived on the other side of town, and I would walk all the way over there just to pass by her house."

"Well, what happened?" I asked.

"She started dating my best friend. I was devastated. I remember thinking that it was the end of the world. But I met Carole the next week," he said. "Now, Carole was something else. She had dark brown hair and green eyes, and she was a cheerleader."

I laughed. My dad seemed more relaxed than I had ever seen him. Maybe my mom was right. She had said that the divorce had made him happier. I smiled. Suddenly I was glad that I had come on this trip with him.

"How is Pam doing?" he asked.

"She's great. She got a new haircut a few weeks ago. It looks super."

"Do you have any classes together?"

"Just homeroom," I said. "But we see each other every day."

"Well, look at that. We're already here," my dad said.

Wow, that drive was quicker than I expected, I thought.

"Are you ready to reel in some whoppers?"

"You bet!" I said. Suddenly I couldn't wait to get out on the boat. This was going to be fun.

We parked the car and took out all of our stuff. I carried the two fishing poles, and my dad carried everything else.

A man was waving at us from the dock. "There's Bob," my dad said.

We walked across a wobbly plank onto the dock. "Well, hello there!" Bob said. "You must be Marci! You're even prettier than your dad said."

I smiled. "Thanks," I said. "Nice to meet you."

"Hey, Dad," a male voice called. "Where's our bunk?"

"Come out here, son," Bob said. He winked at me. "I want you to meet my partner."

A young guy came out of the cabin. My mouth dropped open. There, holding a fishing pole, stood Blue Eyes.

"Dave, this is Marci," Bob said. I looked him straight in the eyes and smiled.

He smiled back.

I held out my hand. "Nice to meet you," I said.

"A pleasure." He laughed, shaking my hand. I got shivers up my back.

"I can't believe you're here," I said. "I thought you'd be at Peter's party."

"I like fishing too much to miss this trip."

"Wow, what a great fishing pole you've got," I said. "How does it work?" I couldn't believe I asked such a dumb question! But Dave smiled and said, "Come on, I'll show you." Then he took my hand and led me onto the boat.

JAN GELMAN is no stranger to writing. She is the daughter of a veteran children's book writer and a magazine journalist, and has spent the last few years as a reporter for *The Vail Trail,* a Colorado newspaper. *Marci's Secret Book of Flirting* was inspired by Ms. Gelman's own personal research that was done for a college paper. The author now lives in New York City and is at work on a second book about Marci's adventures.